BookVenture Publishing LLC
1000 Country Lane Ste 300
Ishpeming MI 49849
www.bookventure.com
Hotline: 1(877) 276-9751
Fax: 1(877) 864-1686

Ordering Information:
Quantity sales. Special discounts are available on quantity purchases by corporations, associations, and others. For details, contact the publisher at the address above.

Printed in the United States of America.

Library of Congress Control Number		2017955630
ISBN-13:	Softcover	978-1-64069-523-8
	Hardcover	978-1-64069-524-5
	Pdf	978-1-64069-525-2
	ePub	978-1-64069-526-9
	Kindle	978-1-64069-527-6

Rev. date: 09/20/17

Audrey's new friend is

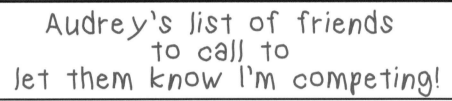

_____

Audrey's list of friends
to call to
let them know I'm competing!

Kahlan	Aspen	Sonali	Mackenzie
Mariana	Anthony	Abi	Sebastian
Lauren	Kimberly	Ashley	Skyla
Dorothy	Richard	Katrina	Katelin
Karen	Chandler	Polina	Faryn
Sofia	Siena	Kinsey	Trysten
Stefan	Delaney	Lucia	Ellie
Jessica	Cheyenne	Yirla	Caroline
Anna	Fynnley	Lilli	Emma
Jonah	Brynn	Brooke	Hadley
Alexandra	Easton	Mady	Izzy

Thank You

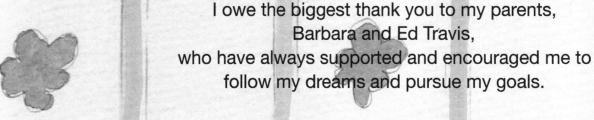

I owe the biggest thank you to my parents,
Barbara and Ed Travis,
who have always supported and encouraged me to
follow my dreams and pursue my goals.

This book would also not have been possible if it weren't for the
support, patience, and understanding of Rodney, my partner
these twenty plus years.

I'd like to express my gratitude to my former coaches Betty Salter,
Peter Burrows, Debbie Milne, Bobbe Shire, Frank Carroll,
Irina Rodnina, Carlow and Christa Fassi, and Peter Oppegard
for their knowledge that helped shape me as a coach.
They have all made a positive difference in my life.

I'd like to thank Nicole Gaboury for her friendship and support.

I'd also like to thank Sheila Thelen for being there at a crucial time
when I needed the push.

My special nieces Clara and Sophia, as well as the students
and families I have been blessed to work with,
have been the true source of inspiration on my journey
into children's book writing. I love you all.

-LT

Audrey's Awesomesauce 1st Competition

Written and Illustrated by **Lance Travis**

"Today is the Day!"
Audrey says

as she opens her eyes and
springs out of bed!

Today is the day of her first
figure skating competition.

She wakes up early and alerts
everyone in the entire house.

"It's my first competition.
We have to get going 'cause
I'm on a mission!"

"I Have to get ready and find my checklist items!"

Can you search Audrey's room and help her find all the items?

Competition Checklist

1. Skates
2. Costume
3. Tights
4. Guards
5. Jacket
6. CD
7. Sneakers
8. Jump rope
9. Makeup
10. Water bottle
11. Tissues
12. Teddy bear
13. Gloves
14. Hair ties

PLEASE REMEMBER!

Audrey rushes down the stairs to have a good breakfast.

Mom says, "Sit down. I've fixed cereal, a waffle, banana, and berries. Chew slowly. We're on time, so no need to worry."

"Can we hurry to the rink now?
Gotta skate, gotta skate!
We can't waste time.
I mustn't be late!"

Awesomesauce Skating Competition

Audrey's coach tells her to arrive at the Awesomesauce Figure Skating Competition one hour before her event starts.

"Wow, look at all the skaters!

I can't wait to practice and compete with them later!"

STRETCH

REACH

Before her event,
Audrey and her coach
do some warm-ups.

Coach tells her to jog
and has her do some
stretching.

Audrey whispers in her coach's ear,

"I'm so nervous!

I have butterflies doing
camel spins in my tummy."

Coach smiles at her
and says, "Being nervous is
normal and okay.

One little word will chase the
butterflies away."

Just use the word "CALM."

Color in a coloring book to ease your mind.

Ask questions so you know what to expect.

Listen to music to relax.

Move your body to shake out the butterflies!

The time comes for Audrey's event. She glides on to the ice to warm up with her friends and competitors.

She runs through all her
skating moves. Swish, swish!
She feels the wind in her hair, as she
spins and flies so swiftly
through the air.

The announcer calls Audrey to the ice. As she performs her program, the butterflies fly away.

She jumps, she spins, and she twirls.

"Wee! Wee! Gliding across the frosty ice, I feel so happy and free!"

"No matter what, I did my best and now it's up to the judges to do the rest!" Audrey exclaims.

Coach reminds her, "Be gracious and kind no matter how you place. Be a good sport and wear a smile on your face."

Everyone waits anxiously
to see how they finished.

Finally, the results are posted on
the wall of the ice rink.

"Yippee! Yippee! The winner is me!"
Audrey cries out.

Friends, Rachael and Bella are
second and third.

They all let out a cheer so that
everyone heard.

At the awards ceremony, Audrey feels so proud.

Her family and friends are clapping for her, as she is presented with her gold medal.

Audrey thanks her coach and
hurries to find her mom.

"I did it! I won!
Will you take us for ice cream now?
It's time for two scoops of fun!"

Mom tells the girls,
"Championship skating
   deserves champion–chip ice cream!"
"We love ice cream almost as much as
   we love ice skating!"
the girls reply with a smile.

"What did you like best about your
first competition?"
Audrey's mother asks.

Audrey thinks back on her awesome,
exciting day.

"Gold medals are great but my
friendships are better. The best thing
about today was friends, and the
time we spent together!"

Friends' Autographs

First Competition

Name/Age: _____ Date: _____

Coach: _____

Competition: _____

Level: _____

Placement: _____

Fondest Competition Memory:

_____

_____

_____

_____

Favorite Ice Cream Flavor: _____

your
picture
here

CPSIA information can be obtained
at www.ICGtesting.com
Printed in the USA
BVIC01n1246211117
500999BV00005B/25

* 9 7 8 1 6 4 0 6 9 5 2 3 8 *